My Friend Ben Won't Share

Charles Beyl

Albert Whitman & Company
Chicago, Illinois

This book is dedicated to Tracy.

Thank you for sharing your life with me.

Library of Congress Cataloging-in-Publication data is on file with the publisher.

Text and illustrations copyright © 2021 by Charles Beyl
First published in the United States of America in 2021 by Albert Whitman & Company
ISBN 978-0-8075-5443-2 (hardcover)
ISBN 978-0-8075-5446-3 (ebook)

Printed in China
10 9 8 7 6 5 4 3 2 1 WKT 24 23 22 21 20

Design by Aphelandra Messer

For more information about Albert Whitman & Company,
visit our website at www.albertwhitman.com.

I'm Chip, and this is my friend Ben.

Ben comes to play at my house.

Ben and I like to swim.
We pretend we are deep-sea divers
hunting for treasure.

We both love to build things.

I build giant forts.

Ben builds the towers for my forts.

Ben likes to write stories.

I like to draw pictures for Ben's stories.

At lunchtime Dad brings us
yummy fern-and-twig sandwiches.

I eat Ben's ferns, and he eats my twigs.

Eating outside with friends is fun.

On sunny days,
we play with our trucks in the sand.

Ben likes my dump truck.

Ben has been playing with my dump truck for a long time.

I want to play with my dump truck.

Ben won't let go.

I pull hard.

Ben pulls hard.

I don't like Ben!

Ben wants to go home.

Maybe he should go home.

If Ben won't share, maybe
Ben shouldn't be my
friend anymore.

I can build forts,
but they won't be as big
without Ben's towers.

Drawing is fun,
but it is more fun drawing
pictures for Ben's stories.

If Ben isn't my friend anymore, who will eat my twigs?

Who will I swim with?
Who will I play trucks with?

Ben is my friend.

I can't wait to see Ben again.

I can't wait to see Ben again.